Buddies for Life

Kaarin Marx-Smith

Perfection Learning®

Illustrator: Dea Marks
Designer: Emily J. Greazel

Dedication

To Rick—You actually lived this story. I merely wrote it.

About the Author

Kaarin Marx-Smith lives in Portland, Oregon, where she shares her passion for writing and "the great outdoors" with her husband and two children. This is her second book.

Contents

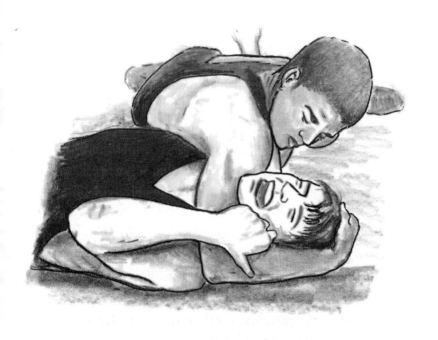

1

No Match for Dad

The moment his shoulder hit the mat, Josh knew it was over.

"One . . . two . . . three . . . He's pinned. That's match!" shouted the referee. Ten seconds. That's how long it had taken the boy from Westview High School to take him down. Ten seconds. It was barely enough time to sneeze, but the humiliation would last a long time.

Josh got up off the mat and congratulated his opponent. He couldn't make out the boy's face, but the stinging defeat didn't blind him from seeing another face in the crowd. His father sat motionless in the bleachers.

Finally Dad had made it to one of my matches, Josh thought. He'd promised to come all season. Well, he'd picked a great night to come. Even from a distance, Josh could read the disappointment on his dad's face.

Josh saw the tall, trim figure of his dad moving down the bleachers toward him. He knew his dad would offer him a ride home. But there was no way Josh wanted to be in the same car as his dad right now. He took a deep breath.

"Hey, Dad . . ."

"Sorry about the match." Mr. Scoville put his hand on his son's shoulders.

"Yeah. Win some—lose some, I guess."

"Ready to go?" his dad asked.

"Coach wants to talk to the whole team in the locker room," Josh stalled. "I'll catch you at home."

"Okay." Mr. Scoville turned to go. "Tough loss, son."

Maybe for you, thought Josh. You never lose. Me? I'm used to it.

The team meeting after the tournament was just like all the others. The coach directed most of his comments to the varsity wrestlers. Fortunately, most of them had won their matches, so his words were positive. JV wrestlers like Josh—especially those who had lost—were pretty much ignored. Josh was grateful. He didn't want any more attention called to his humiliating defeat than was necessary.

Actually, Josh thought, he hadn't had a bad season overall. He'd won several of his matches. But, of course, his dad hadn't been there for those.

Joining the wrestling team had seemed like a good idea last fall. Josh had been so excited that night at dinner when he'd announced that he'd made Glencoe's JV team.

"Nice work," his dad had said proudly. "I wrestled a bit in high school myself—middleweight class."

Over Christmas vacation, Josh had dreamed of the referee raising his arm, loudly declaring him a winner. His dad had been in the bleachers smiling proudly at his son. Somehow Josh had never imagined the scene he'd just lived today. Losing in front of his dad was his worst nightmare.

"Ready to take off?" His friend Matt snapped a towel, interrupting his thoughts.

"Yeah, sure, let me grab my things." Josh stuffed his gear into a faded blue gym bag. Then he grabbed his skateboard from his locker.

Neither Josh nor Matt was old enough to drive. Skateboarding was their main form of transportation. The two boys had mapped out a route home. First they flew down the steps of the city library. Then they kicked over some tracks from the commuter rail line. Their ride ended with an exhilarating sail down "Dead Man's Hill."

Once home, they'd usually practice a few half-pipes and twists. They'd built a ramp in front of Josh's house. Josh loved the rush that came with skateboarding. He also loved the way boarding required total concentration. When he was on his skateboard, the rest of the world was a million miles away.

On the ride home, all thoughts of wrestling disappeared. Matt and Josh were out front practicing some new moves when Josh's mom opened the front door.

"Josh, it's time for dinner," she called out.

"Gotta go," he muttered to his friend.

Dinner at the Scoville house was a serious affair. Both his parents insisted that Josh and his younger sister, Amber, always be present. Exceptions were occasionally made for Josh's older brother. Sean started on the Glencoe High School basketball team and sometimes had to practice late. But even those exceptions were rare.

"Hey, what's the matter?" Matt asked. "Your mom's a great cook. So is your dad, actually." Matt grinned.

Matt was right. Both his parents were great cooks. Josh used to love eating with his family. Lately, however, he was beginning to dread family dinners.

"I'm beginning to feel like *I'm* the meal," Josh groaned.

"Huh?"

"Well, dad grills me so much about what I'm doing—or *not* doing—that I might as well be the barbecue he likes to fix."

"Yeah, that's tough," answered Matt slowly. "But it would be nice to *have* a dad to hang with once in a while." Matt's dad lived in another state. He didn't spend much time with Matt or his younger sister.

"Hang out with my dad?" Josh grimaced. "Get hung out to dry is more like it. Seems like I'm always in trouble."

Matt just shrugged.

"Well, catch you later," Josh said.

"Yeah, later. Hang tough." Matt's curly red hair fell into his eyes as he skated away.

The rest of the family was already seated when Josh reached the kitchen. The sunny yellow room did nothing to improve his mood.

His mom patted his shoulders as he sat down at the table. "Dad told me about your match. I'm sorry," she said.

Sean, his older brother by two years, passed Josh the lasagna. Then he turned back to his dad. "Our team isn't going to let anyone get inside. It's outside the key that we have to worry about."

"Yeah, I think Coach Redmond needs to pull you guys back. Especially if you're going to have a chance against Lincoln tomorrow night. They have two really good long-range shooters," Mr. Scoville said.

As usual, the conversation at dinner centered around basketball. For once, Josh was grateful. He ate in silence while Sean and his dad discussed tomorrow night's game.

Suddenly Mr. Scoville turned to his daughter. "Amber, what was the best thing that happened to you today?"

Josh sighed. He used to look forward to his dad's routine dinner question. Every night, his dad asked each of them what had been the best thing to happen that day. When he was little, Josh had waited all day to share his "best thing." Sometimes it had been hard to wait his turn. As he'd gotten older, it had just become more of a routine thing that he put up with. These days, Josh was torn. He wasn't really interested in sharing his life with his family, but he did wish that his dad would care enough to ask.

Josh pretended to be interested in Amber's reply. She was a good kid, but Josh didn't usually pay much attention to her. Amber was only in third grade, so she still got excited about sharing her "best thing."

"I got my Reading Star Award for reading so many books," she was saying now. "I get to have lunch in a restaurant next week with Mrs. Bauer, my reading teacher. I was the first one in my class to read all the books on the list." Amber grinned proudly.

"That's my girl," Mr. Scoville praised.

Then he turned to Josh. "Please pass the lasagna. It sure hits the spot tonight."

That was it, Josh thought. He'd been passed over like the evening's lasagna. In this family, if you didn't win, you didn't get noticed.

He wanted to scream. The conversation swirled around his head. Occasionally someone tried to draw him in. He could have joined in if he'd wanted to. He could have been part of the family. Instead he went someplace else inside his head.

Josh pushed the lasagna around on his plate. He didn't feel hungry. He knew his dad was disappointed in him. He hadn't just witnessed a loss that afternoon. He'd seen his son go down in humiliating defeat.

Don't worry, though, Dad, Josh thought bitterly. It's not catching.

Part of him wanted his dad to acknowledge the match in some way. Had he even seen it? Or had Josh just imagined that his dad had been there? Maybe he was so disappointed that he couldn't even talk about it.

A feeling of rejection washed over Josh. It was even stronger than the humiliation he'd felt on the mat that afternoon.

"Josh . . . Josh." It was Sean. "Hey, Josh, do you want your dessert? If you're not going to eat it, I will."

"Go ahead," Josh mumbled. He took his half-eaten plate of lasagna to the sink and headed up to his room.

"What's bugging him?" he heard Sean ask.

2
Life Is a Jigsaw Puzzle

In the eyes of an adult, Josh's room could be labeled a pigsty. Clothes lay on the floor. The bed was unmade. Unsuccessful homework attempts were crumpled on the carpet around his desk.

His parents had let him paint the walls midnight blue. Then Josh had covered them with extreme skateboarding and snowboarding posters.

Now he turned on his computer and stereo, hoping to drown out reality. Drumming his fingers on the keyboard, Josh tried to forget about his dad's rejection.

He figured he might as well get a head start on his weekend homework. He was writing a biology term paper on the destruction of coral reefs. Logging on to the Internet, he was soon lost in a sea of screens. An underwater world of brilliantly colored coral and interesting sea creatures sprang to life. He was so fascinated with his research that he didn't hear the quiet knock at his door.

"Hey, can I come in?" His mom finally peeked her head in when Josh didn't respond to her knock. It wasn't unusual for her to drop by his room after dinner. She was a magazine writer and sometimes helped him with his writing homework.

"Sure, if you don't say anything about the clothes on the bed," Josh said.

"What about the dishes on the floor?" His mom sighed and shook her head. She cleared a space on the bed and sat down.

Josh closed a few screens on his computer. Then he turned around to look at her. Her brown hair was swept back into a ponytail. In an oversized sweater and jeans, she looked more like one of his friends than his mom.

"What are you working on?" she asked.

"A paper on how we're destroying the world's coral reefs."

"Coral reefs, huh?" said Mrs. Scoville. "Your dad and I did some diving together in Malaysia right after we were married. They had some fabulous reefs."

"Not anymore," Josh told her.

"That's too bad," she said thoughtfully. "They were really beautiful."

Then she changed the subject. "Hey, I know your dad can be rough on you sometimes."

"Try *all* the time," Josh interrupted.

His mom sighed. She felt caught between her husband and son. She had cringed at dinner when her husband had passed over Josh. She knew the insult hadn't been intentional. Her husband just hadn't wanted to humiliate Josh further. How could he know that ignoring Josh would make him feel even worse?

Mrs. Scoville put her hand on Josh's knee. He's almost as big as his father, she thought. Another growth spurt and Josh would pass her six-foot husband.

"For some people, life just seems to come easily, doesn't it?" she said finally. "They know what they want, and they go after it. Everything falls into place like the pieces of a jigsaw puzzle.

"For your dad, life is one big adventure. He's been successful at everything he's ever tried. He doesn't really understand failure. And he doesn't understand that there are some good lessons to be learned from losing. It makes you strong and more determined. It also helps you to see things from the other guy's point of view."

Josh just shrugged.

"Your dad didn't mean to hurt you tonight," his mom continued. "He wasn't intentionally ignoring you. He just didn't know what to say." She laughed. "I guess that's where *he* fails, isn't it?"

His mom stood up. "Anyway, the movie is about to start, and the popcorn is ready."

Josh followed his mom down the stairs to the family room. This was their thing. Almost every Friday night, Josh and his mom curled up in front of the TV with a bowl of popcorn and watched movies. Dad usually headed to the bedroom to read. Sean went out with friends, and Amber was too young to stay up so late.

Josh and his mom sat on the couch. The bowl of popcorn rested between them. Watching the movie, Josh imagined that he was the hero. He wished he were a hero in real life—someone people looked up to and went to for help. Someone who wasn't a loser.

Keep dreaming, he told himself. You're certainly no hero.

3
Too Much Family

Josh woke up the next morning still stinging from the brush-off he'd gotten at dinner the night before. He went downstairs and grabbed breakfast. His mom was hustling Amber out the door to her gymnastics class.

"Good morning," she called from the doorway. "Don't forget that you promised Mrs. Jenks you'd mow her lawn."

Josh groaned. He'd forgotten all about it.
Gulping down the rest of his orange juice, he
headed out the door. Mrs. Jenks lived a few houses
up the block. He could hear his dad and Sean
playing a game of one-on-one in the driveway.

"That was a foul, and you know it," his dad
called out.

"If that was a foul, then I'm Shaquille O'Neal,"
Sean responded.

"Man, your reffing is on vacation."

"Dad, your whole game has taken a vacation."
Sean laughed. He drove around his dad for a layup.

"Nice shot." Mr. Scoville was breathing hard
but grinning.

Josh watched the game for a second more
before heading up the street. He knocked on
Mrs. Jenks' door. She answered and led Josh to the
garage where she stored her ancient push mower.

As the blades of the mower whirred across the
lawn, Josh made a plan. Between now and dinner,
he was going to have to find an excuse not to go to
Sean's game tonight. After yesterday's wrestling
match, he didn't think he could sit through four
quarters of his family cheering wildly for his brother.

Josh could just imagine the scene. Lincoln would
be ahead by two points with four seconds left on the
clock. A teammate would pass the ball to Sean. He'd
go up for the three-point shot. His mom's hands

would be over her eyes. His dad would be out of his
seat. Amber would be hoarse from yelling. Swish.
The buzzer would sound. The game would end in
another win for the great Sean Scoville.

"Always the hero," Josh muttered.

Afterward the whole family would celebrate with
ice cream around the kitchen table. But that was
one party Josh could miss. He'd had a little too
much family lately.

Josh called Matt on the phone as soon as he was
finished mowing.

"How's it going?" he asked when Matt answered.

"Good. What's up with you?" Matt replied.

"Not much. I was kind of hoping we could hang
together tonight. Maybe I could spend the night?"

"That's not gonna work. Mom has a date, so I
have to watch Desiree. You know my mom won't let
me have friends over when she's gone. Sorry."

"No problem," Josh said. He hung up the phone
and banged his head lightly against the wall. Now he
needed a new plan.

Just then, Mrs. Scoville walked in the back door.
She was juggling an armload of groceries. Setting
the bags on the counter, she looked at Josh.

"Can you grab a bag of groceries from the car?"

"Yeah, sure, Mom." He headed out the door.
When he returned, she looked up from the fridge.
"How did things go with Mrs. Jenks?"

"Fine. Uh, Mom, do you mind if I head over to Matt's tonight? We're working on a project together for history."

"Josh, you know Sean has a game tonight."

"Yeah, I know, but the project's due Monday. We really have to study."

"Well, okay. But, Josh," she said, smiling, "you're not fooling me with that studying bit. Have fun tonight, and don't stay out too late."

"Thanks, Mom," Josh said, sighing in relief. He'd actually gotten away with it!

4
Beginner's Luck

Josh watched Amber and his parents climb into the family's ancient green van and drive to the game. He grabbed his backpack. His mom thought it was full of books—not the food and sweatshirt that were really in it. Josh hopped on his skateboard and headed in the opposite direction of the school. Instead of stopping at Matt's house, he kept going.

At first, Josh didn't really know where he was headed. He just knew that he was free. Crossing a few more streets, he realized he'd be downtown soon. He and Matt had ridden along the river parkway that wound through downtown many times. But he'd never been downtown by himself at night before.

A red steel bridge with metal gratings separated his neighborhood of Victorian homes from the modern skyscrapers lining downtown. Josh crossed over the bridge.

It was a chilly but clear Saturday evening near the end of February. The day had been unseasonably warm, which had brought people outside. Josh found himself winding his way through large groups of kids just hanging out. Couples walked along the river.

Finally he came to the Market Street Fountain at the end of the riverfront. Water sprung up from the bottom of the fountain. Stubby concrete posts containing colored lights circled the spouting water.

The fountain was a gathering place for kids and adults. When Josh had been younger, his parents had brought picnic lunches to eat on the grassy lawn nearby. He and Sean had raced through the ribbons of water.

Tonight, teenagers rode their mountain bikes or skateboards through the water. Josh zigzagged a few times around the lit-up posts. He felt a million miles away from his family.

After a few more times around the fountain, Josh kicked up his board and walked toward the river. Two sets of stairs trailed down to a concrete dock. There, several recreational boats and a dinner cruise ship were tied up. A handful of high school kids had built a small ramp on the dock. They were doing skateboard tricks down the stairs.

Josh thought he'd watch the action for a while. After a few minutes, his body started twitching. He wanted to join the fun. He was eager to show the kids what he could do with a few stairs. Josh grabbed his board.

"Mind if I take a turn?" he asked a husky teen with black hair and long sideburns. The kid seemed older than the rest of the group. Josh figured he was the leader.

"No problem," the boy drawled.

Josh started down the slight incline of the parkway, gathering speed as he went. With both hands holding on to his board, he jumped the railing separating the river from the walkway. Board and boy rode across the steel railing like a train on its track. Then they separated, meeting up again on the stairs. Josh hopped the last three steps on his board and finished up at the feet of the leader.

"Not bad," the boy grunted.

Josh just shrugged, but inside he felt great. He had nailed that trick, and he knew it.

Josh also knew he should head home. It was dark now. Only the stars and streetlights lit the city. His mom would freak if she knew he was riding his skateboard alone in the dark.

Josh wanted to hold on to the moment a bit longer though. He took a couple of breaths of cold air. Here on the river walk, he was a million miles away from the crowd of high school basketball fans celebrating its heroes.

The crowd began to thin. Josh kicked up his board and turned to go.

"Hey!" It was the leader. "My name's Max. Want to hang for a while?"

Josh hesitated only a moment. "Yeah, sure."

The group started walking toward the city center. Josh figured they were headed to the main square. A lot of kids hung out there. They listened to music, played hacky sack, or just watched people. Josh and his friends had always felt like outsiders. Sometimes they would check out the scene from afar, but they never joined in.

Max picked up a few stones from the gutter. He threw a couple of them up at a streetlight and missed. Next a scrawny kid with spiky bleached hair threw a stone. He dinged the lamp, but the rock bounced off without damaging the light. Max handed a couple of rocks to Josh. Without thinking, Josh tossed one toward a light. Smash. The tinkling sound of breaking glass filled the air. For a second, it was completely silent as a circle of darkness surrounded the broken light.

Then the group continued walking.

"Nice aim," Max said. "Or else it's beginner's luck." Max handed Josh another rock. "Here, try again."

"Sure, why not?" Josh replied. He took the rock and tossed it up. Smash. Apparently he was better at this than he knew.

The group moved on. They were following Josh now. He was up front with Max. His step felt a little more confident. Unconsciously, Josh threw his shoulders back and walked to the next light post. "Two down and one to go," he said to himself.

Josh knew he was pushing his luck. He knew his parents would kill him if they found out. But the temptation to throw just one more rock was overwhelming. He lifted his arm slightly and flicked his wrist. The sound of the police siren coincided with the sound of glass shattering on the pavement. The light went out.

Instead of total darkness, however, the street was suddenly bathed in bright light. Kids scattered quickly—except Josh. He was frozen in the blinding headlights of a police car.

5
Skip the Party

Josh tried to find comfort in the fact that there had been no family ice cream party to celebrate another basketball victory. The sight of Josh being escorted up the front steps of his house by a police officer had dampened any party plans. Amber was sent up to her room. Sean was told to be quiet.

As Josh had sat in the backseat of the squad car, he'd wondered what his parents would say.

Unfortunately, the scene had played out almost exactly as he'd predicted. It had been brutal. The officer had explained that Josh would have to pay for the damaged streetlights by doing community service. Even worse than the punishment had been the look on his dad's face.

"He'll pay all right," his father said grimly.

"Because it's his first offense, there won't be any charges filed this time," the officer explained.

"I can assure you, officer," said Mr. Scoville, "that there will be no next time."

"I hope not," the officer said, turning to go.

The door closed behind the police officer. Mr. Scoville turned to face his son. He could barely contain his rage. His dad spoke calmly, but Josh could see the veins in his neck bulging.

"What were you thinking, Josh? What?" his dad asked. He slammed a fist into the palm of his other hand over and over again.

For a moment, Josh couldn't answer. Then something inside him burst.

"I was *thinking* that maybe I'd rather spend my time with some people who don't think I'm a loser!" he exploded. "I know that you would never have done something so terrible, but I'm not you. No one could possibly be as perfect as you are."

"That's enough," his dad cut him off. "Here's the deal. You're grounded for three months. No skateboarding. No wrestling. No friends. Nothing. You walk home. You go to your room. You do your homework. Of course, you'll also do your community service. That's it for the next three months. After that, we'll talk. Now get upstairs."

An hour later, Josh's mom knocked on his door. When he didn't answer, his mom walked in. She was still wearing her blue and yellow Glencoe Viking sweatshirt. Josh was lying on his bed, staring up at the ceiling.

"Do you want to talk about it?" she asked quietly. "It's not like you. I'm disappointed."

"Well, stand in line!" he snapped.

She sighed. "Come on, Josh. Don't tell me you're not disappointed in yourself. You know better. But until you figure out who you are and accept it, you'll keep being disappointed."

"Yeah, right," Josh muttered. But inside he had a sneaking suspicion that she was right.

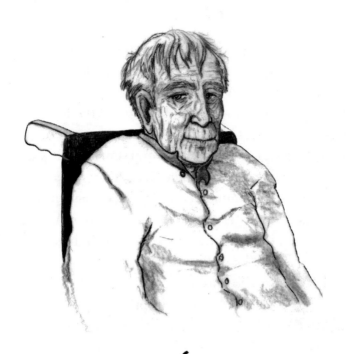

6
Evergreen Terrace

Three days later, Josh started his community service. He hated it.

The Youth Offender's Officer had placed him at Evergreen Terrace. "It's close to your school, so you'll be able to walk," he told a sullen Josh.

Josh had never even noticed the nursing home before. Now there was no way he'd ever forget it. He worked there every afternoon until his dad picked him up.

The beige walls and crummy green linoleum floors became more familiar to him than his own bedroom. He could never get used to the smell that washed over him every time he entered the home. He called it "the old people smell."

Josh thought working at Evergreen Terrace was a lot worse than being grounded at home. Most of the residents sat slumped over in wheelchairs in the hall outside their rooms. A few even drooled. When Josh passed the old men and women with their stringy hair and loose-fitting pajamas, some of them would reach out to grasp his hand.

Josh always felt the urge to sprint from the front door to the janitor's closet. But he couldn't afford to get into more trouble, so he slowed his pace. Keeping his eyes on the floor, he avoided the residents in the hallway.

Each day before he began, Josh had to check in with Mr. DeSilva. Mr. DeSilva was the home's janitor and Josh's boss.

The routine never varied. Josh would grab the mop and bucket from the janitor's closet. Then he'd start washing the old linoleum floor in the dining room. Next he had to clean the public restrooms. After that, he could take a 20-minute break.

Josh would race outside for some fresh air. Usually he'd sit on one of the benches set out for the residents. They rarely used them.

Sometimes he'd go across the street to the small shopping center and buy a pop and some chips. Then he'd head back to the bench to eat his snack.

He'd been working at Evergreen Terrace for several weeks now. Today was the first day of spring. The blue sky was cloudless. A light breeze stirred the warm air. It was a perfect day to be outside. Not that anyone at Evergreen Terrace would notice. They were all inside. Josh would have given anything to be skateboarding with Matt instead of mopping floors.

It's not fair, he thought bitterly. I make one little mistake, and I have to pay for it by working here.

"Sean probably wouldn't even have gotten caught," Josh mumbled out loud to himself.

He looked at his watch. Time to head back in for the rest of his shift. He crumpled up his empty bag and tossed it into the garbage can. Score. Two points.

Slowly he made his way into the nursing home. It was time to mop the hallways. On his way to the janitor's closet, he passed an elderly man sitting in a wheelchair. The man was fumbling with his watch. He struggled to put it on. Finally the watch dropped to the floor. Josh leaned over and picked it up. He handed the ancient gold watch back to the man.

"Thanks," the old man growled.

"You're welcome," Josh replied in an equally unfriendly tone. Man, I hate this place, he thought. Even the people who live here hate it.

He started mopping the hallway. Out of the corner of his eye, he watched the old man try to comb his hair. All the buttons on his pajama top were undone. Why wasn't anyone helping him? The old man might be a jerk, but he didn't need to be humiliated. Finally Josh couldn't take it anymore.

He put his mop down and walked over to the man. "Do you need some help?" he asked.

"What if I do?" the old man grumbled irritably.

"Sorry, just trying to help." Josh backed away.

The old man hesitated. "Here." He handed Josh the comb. "It's Thursday, and my daughter is coming to visit."

"Might want to do something about those buttons," Josh mumbled under his breath.

The old man heard him. "I know," he said. Then he shook his head sadly. "My fingers don't work too well since my stroke."

Josh was embarrassed. "Here, let me help. There. That's much better."

With his shirt buttoned and his hair combed, the old man looked much better. He almost looks like Granddad, thought Josh.

Josh knew he'd better get back to his mopping. Mr. DeSilva wouldn't be happy if he caught him slacking. As he turned to pick up the mop, he said, "My name is Josh, by the way."

"Humph" was the man's only response.

Josh's mind wandered as he listened to the swish, swish, swish of the mop. What was it like to live here? It seemed lonely and depressing. He hoped he never had to live in a place like this.

The sound of a horn honking in the parking lot brought Josh back to the present. He quickly finished the area he was mopping. Then he shoved the equipment back in the closet.

"Gotta go. My dad's here," he called to Mr. DeSilva on his way out.

"See you tomorrow," Mr. DeSilva said.

"Yeah, unfortunately," Josh retorted as he raced out the door.

"How's it going?" Mr. Scoville asked as Josh slid into the front seat and slammed the door.

"All right," Josh mumbled.

"Glad to hear it." His dad turned on the radio. Josh hated his dad's taste in music. However, he was glad they wouldn't have to talk. Any music was better than their silence and awkwardness. That was the way the car rides had been lately. That was the way everything had been lately—silent and awkward.

The only good thing about Evergreen Terrace was that it gave him an escape from his dad and the silence. At the nursing home, no one paid much attention to him. He just did his own thing and no one cared. That was a lot easier than trying to please his dad.

Mr. DeSilva had tried drawing him out by cracking corny jokes. At first Josh didn't bite, but slowly he'd begun to lighten up. Mr. DeSilva was just trying to make the best of a bad situation, Josh realized. Then he began to realize that wasn't true either. Mr. DeSilva genuinely liked the place. He chatted with the residents. He asked them about their kids or grandkids. He actually cared.

Josh wondered if Mr. DeSilva knew the old man he had helped today. He reminded himself to ask him tomorrow.

"Who's that man who always sits in the hallway waiting for his daughter?" Josh asked Mr. DeSilva the next day.

"Oh, that's Mr. Ryan," Mr. DeSilva replied. "He used to be a big banker here in town."

"He did?" Josh was astonished. "You'd never know it to look at him now."

"No," Mr. DeSilva shook his head sadly. "His daughter is all he has now. That's more than a lot of people in this place have though. Of course, they all have me," he joked. "And you. Although you aren't much to look at right now all covered in grime."

"Thanks a lot," Josh said, smiling.

After his break, Josh stopped by Mr. Ryan.

"How's it going?" he asked. "I brought you some chips." Feeling awkward, he shoved the bag at the old man.

"Potato chips?" Mr. Ryan hesitated. He said slowly, "It's been a long time, but I bet they still taste the same. Thank you."

"You're welcome," Josh said, staring at the floor. "Well, I'd better get back to work." He took off down the hall.

After that, it became easier to talk to the old man. The conversations were never long, but they were less and less awkward. Sometimes Mr. Ryan would wordlessly hand Josh his comb. Often the boy would silently button the top of Mr. Ryan's pajamas.

One day, the old man wheeled up to Josh wearing an ancient suit jacket over his pajamas. Josh started to laugh. Then he stopped when he realized how different Mr. Ryan looked. He was starting to look more like the important bank president he had once been. It wasn't because of the jacket, though, but because he had regained his dignity.

His friendship with Mr. Ryan had changed Josh too. He no longer dreaded his days at Evergreen Terrace. And it became easier for him to smile at the other residents as he passed them in the hall. Sometimes he even stopped to help them with something.

His breaks became less important. Sometimes he would even stay inside to talk to Mr. Ryan.

One day, Josh spent his break in Mr. Ryan's room. While they were talking, he noticed some medals lying on a dresser.

"Where'd you get those medals?" Josh asked.

"I fought in World War II. That's where I got the watch too." Mr. Ryan paused for a moment, lost in his memories. Then he spoke quietly.

"I was part of the troops that first liberated France. An old French woman came up and handed the watch to me. Tears streamed down her face. She was so happy that the Americans had arrived."

Josh noticed that Mr. Ryan's eyes looked misty as he told his story.

"The woman said the watch was her most prized possession. She'd kept it buried in her backyard for years. She gave it to me as a thank-you for her freedom. Nothing was more important to her than that."

"You were her hero," Josh said.

"A hero? No. I was just doing my job like thousands of other soldiers. I'm proud of what we did. You don't have to be a hero to make a difference."

"Speaking of making a difference . . ." Mr. DeSilva stepped into the room. "How about you making a difference on these floors?" He handed Josh a mop. His voice sounded serious, but he was smiling.

"Nothing I could do to these floors could possibly make a difference—except maybe replacing them," Josh shot back. He took the mop, though, and got to work.

France Gives Our Boys a Heroes' Welcome

7

No Heroes Here

The next morning, Josh woke up in an empty house. His mom and Amber were off at gymnastics. He had no idea where his dad and brother were. Josh sat at the kitchen table drinking his juice and gazing out the window.

Spring had come, and he'd been too busy to notice. Now he saw the burst of color in his dad's garden. Bright yellow and red tulips mingled happily with purple irises. Even a few branches of pink dogwood were still blooming. Josh had to admit that his dad had a way with flowers—if you were into that sort of thing. The burst of color in the backyard made the drizzly March morning seem less gloomy.

An idea started to form in the back of Josh's mind. He finished his juice and headed outside. Grabbing the garden clippers from the garage, he scanned the backyard. First he cut some tulips. There were so many, he figured his dad wouldn't notice if a few were missing. Then he clipped some dogwood branches. They were almost done blooming anyway.

"Hey, what are you doing?" His dad's voice startled Josh. He whirled around. For a second, he was afraid his dad was angry. Josh quickly explained his idea to his dad. A slow smile spread across Mr. Scoville's face.

"Mind if I help?" his dad asked. "Let's add a few of these irises while we're at it."

The guys worked together in silence. But for once, it wasn't an awkward silence. It was peaceful.

Finally Josh said, "That's enough. I'll take them over now."

"Let me drive you."

"Sure, that would be great."

Minutes later, the two arrived at Evergreen Terrace. Josh's dad had never actually been inside the nursing home. He just dropped Josh off and picked him up outside.

Today, however, he followed Josh cautiously. Mr. Scoville would never admit it, but he'd always felt a little uncomfortable around old people. He never knew what to say or what to do. Now he watched in surprise as his son moved easily down the hallway. Josh greeted everyone. He even stopped to straighten a shirt and pick up a dropped book.

Since when had Josh become friends with these people? his dad wondered. He hadn't even noticed Josh's change in attitude toward his community service.

When they got to the dining room, Josh grabbed a couple of empty coffee cans from the kitchen. He started filling them with water. He didn't know much about flower arranging, so he just stuffed the flowers into the makeshift vases.

"Dad, can you put these on the tables out in the dining room?"

Mr. Scoville grabbed the cans. Soon all the flowers were on the tables. Josh and his dad stood in the doorway admiring their work.

"Well, that certainly brightens things up in here," Mr. Scoville said.

"Yeah, it can get pretty dismal sometimes," Josh added.

"Dad," he said suddenly, "there's someone I want you to meet." Mr. Ryan had rolled into the dining room.

"So this is your dad," Mr. Ryan said. "Pleased to meet you. You have a real fine son there."

"Thank you, sir." Mr. Scoville couldn't think of anything else to say.

Mr. Ryan went on, "Josh, it looks like you've been busy. The flowers sure look pretty."

"Thanks, Mr. Ryan. Well, we'd better be going. See you Monday." Josh took the old man's hand for a moment. Then he dropped it quickly. He wasn't sure what his dad would think.

The ride home was quiet. Josh stared out the window, lost in thought. Why couldn't his own dad be as proud of him as Mr. Ryan was?

When Josh showed up for work on Monday, Mr. Ryan wasn't waiting for him in the hallway. Instead, the director of the nursing home met him.

"I have some sad news for you, Josh," the director said. "Mr. Ryan died in his sleep Saturday night."

Josh didn't say anything, so the director continued.

"He left this for you." The director handed Josh a yellowed newspaper clipping and Mr. Ryan's ancient gold watch. Josh looked at the clipping. The headline read "France Gives Our Boys a Hero's Welcome." A photo showed several American soldiers handing out gum and chocolate to a group of French children. Josh looked closer. One of the soldiers was wearing a gold watch exactly like the one he held in his hand.

Josh was quiet for a moment. "Guess I'd better get to work," he finally said.

Josh was numb as he dragged the mop across the dirty linoleum. He could hardly wait for his break. He had to get out of there. He couldn't breathe. For the first time in weeks, he felt trapped in the nursing home.

When his break finally did arrive, Josh ran across the street to the shopping center. He wandered through the shops, not really looking at anything. Nothing interested him now.

Mr. Ryan wasn't the first person Josh knew that had died. His grandmother had died a couple of years ago. He'd been sad and had even cried. But this was different. Mr. Ryan had been his friend. Friends weren't supposed to leave you.

Josh looked at the watch that Mr. Ryan had left him. He still had a few more minutes before he had to go back to work. He decided to explore the small scuba diving shop. He'd noticed it before but had never gone in.

Josh stepped into the shop. He gazed at the bright yellow air tanks, the mask and snorkel sets, and the wet suits hanging along a wall. He wasn't all that familiar with scuba diving. He knew his dad had done a lot of diving as a Navy Seal. Josh had seen his equipment in the basement. When was the last time his dad had actually used the stuff?

For a moment, the thought of his dad ruined the idea of learning to scuba dive. But then again, Josh thought, maybe if I learned how to dive, my dad would pay some attention to me.

Josh glanced down at his watch. He was late! He turned to go. As he headed out the door, his eye caught a notice on the bulletin board.

Josh was intrigued. His interest in the ocean had definitely grown since he'd started researching coral reefs. Maybe this was an opportunity to explore a world he'd only read about. Josh grabbed one of the flyers before heading back to the nursing home.

Scuba Diving Classes

Sign up now.
Classes start soon.

Explore the world under the sea this summer.

Later that evening, Josh thought about the scuba lessons again. He didn't know whether his parents would let him do it. They hadn't let him do much since his brush with the law. His community service was almost over though. He'd have more free time. And he could use his savings from mowing Mrs. Jenks' lawn to pay for the classes.

I wonder if Matt would be interested in taking the classes with me? Josh mused as he drifted off to sleep.

Josh bumped into Matt on his way to algebra. Matt thought the idea sounded fun.

"Diving's a real adventure sport. And I bet there will be lots of hot girls hanging out at the beach. I'll have to ask my mom first though."

"Yeah, me too," said Josh. "My dad probably won't even let me do it. I'll call you tonight after I ask."

The two boys separated at the door of Josh's classroom. While his teacher droned on about x and y equations, Josh imagined swimming in the warm waters of the Caribbean. He had visions of barracudas, moray eels, and octopuses darting in and out of coral reefs.

That night at dinner, Josh brought up the subject of scuba lessons. His parents reacted better than he'd expected.

"You've done a good job of keeping your nose clean these past few months," his dad said. "I think you've learned some valuable lessons."

"If this is something you really want to do, then we'll support you," his mom added. "Your dad used to love diving."

She looked over at her husband. "Maybe he'll pick it up again someday."

"No way I'd want to dive," Sean broke in.

"Yeah," Amber piped up, "remember when you got stung by a jellyfish in Hawaii?"

"I do." Mrs. Scoville frowned. "The whole beach knew Sean had been stung. He was yelling at the top of his lungs."

"You would have thought he'd been attacked by a great white shark, not some silly old jellyfish," laughed Amber.

"It wasn't like that at all." Sean was turning red.

"Well, you've never been one to just jump in the water since then," his dad admitted.

Actually, Josh knew Sean was terrified of water. His brother had been dying to be a lifeguard this summer and have girls falling all over him. However, he couldn't bring himself to take a lifesaving class. Even the thought of hanging out with cheerleaders at the pool all summer couldn't get Sean in the water.

"Tell us about a time when you went diving, Dad," Amber piped up.

"I remember lots of big, colorful fish," Mr. Scoville said. "But I think the most fun I've had diving was with your mom. We were in a shallow lagoon. Dozens of manta rays started swimming around us. They were so gentle. Remember that, Gabby?"

"I do remember," Josh's mom said. "I also remember the shark that followed them into the lagoon."

"That's right. Your mom hid behind me until it swam away." He laughed. The family listened eagerly. It reminded Josh of how things used to be.

His dad smiled at Josh. "It sure would feel good to get my scuba gear on and go underwater again. Maybe we could be dive buddies."

Josh wasn't sure about that. Be "buddies" with his dad? He couldn't even imagine it.

8
Buddy Breathing

Matt and Josh started their scuba diving classes a few weeks later. They were disappointed when their instructor, Chris, told the students that they would have several "dry-land sessions" first. They would only be allowed to put on scuba gear and get into the water after these sessions.

Josh had thought scuba diving was going to be an adventure sport, not more school. He had trouble keeping his mind on what Chris was saying. His brain hurt. He wanted to get into the water.

Don't hold your breath underwater! Chris wrote on the chalkboard.

"Why not?" one of the girls in the class burst out.

"Let me show you," Chris said. He placed a clear plastic bottle of pop on the counter. The class just stared at it, waiting for an explanation.

"What gives pop its fizz?" Chris asked.

"Carbonated water," Josh replied.

"Yes," Chris agreed. "And carbonated water is water with a little carbon dioxide gas added."

Chris held up the bottle for the class to see.

"Why don't we see all the bubbles when the bottle is sealed?" he asked.

No one answered.

"You can't see the bubbles because the bottle is under a lot of pressure," Chris explained. "But when I unscrew the cap, what happens?"

"The bubbles escape," Matt said.

"Exactly!" Chris said. "When I open the cap, I relieve the pressure. Then the bubbles—the carbon dioxide gas—can escape."

"What does this have to do with scuba diving?" Josh asked.

"Think of your body as a bottle of pop. The deeper you dive, the more pressure the water creates around your body. We don't notice that pressure because we're breathing air from our tanks. If we rise to the surface of the water slowly and breathing normally, the bubbles of nitrogen gas that have built up in our bodies have time to escape."

Chris took the bottle of pop and shook it hard. He opened it. Pop sprayed everywhere. The class stared at him in shock.

"*That*," Chris said, "is what happens if a diver surfaces too quickly. The nitrogen bubbles don't have time to escape. The pressure is tremendous. The gas can damage your heart and lungs. Make sense?"

The class nodded in understanding.

"Great," Chris said. "Now help me clean up this mess!"

"You'll be in the water soon enough," his dad said when Josh complained that night at dinner. "It's important to understand how to breathe underwater. Both you and your buddy will depend on it."

"I know, but don't I have to *get* underwater to worry about breathing under it?" Josh moaned.

"You'll be glad you know this stuff later," his dad reminded him. Josh listened carefully as his dad went over the importance of correct underwater breathing.

Josh's dad had been right. The class did get into the water soon enough. And when they did, Josh wished that he'd paid more attention to the lectures. There was so much to think about underwater. Josh felt an odd mixture of fear and excitement.

First the class practiced finding their breathing rhythm underwater. Once he mastered that, Josh was able to look around as he swam. But since they were "diving" in a swimming pool, there wasn't much to look at besides the faces of his classmates. Josh was looking forward to diving in the ocean.

He watched a steady stream of bubbles rise to the water's surface. He listened to the slow, rhythmic sound of his own breathing as he sucked air from the tank strapped to his back. In. Out. In. Out.

He was still not quite used to breathing through the regulator. The idea of depending on a mouthpiece and hose connected to an air tank for his next breath took a little getting used to. But the regulator was what allowed divers to breathe comfortably even at great depths.

After a while, the soft, slow sound of the regulator amplifying his breathing was actually kind of relaxing. Kicking his fins, he glided smoothly through the water.

Suddenly, Matt, who was his dive buddy, slashed a finger across his throat. It was the signal that he was running out of air.

Josh knew that meant he was supposed to give Matt some of his air. Josh remembered what he'd learned in class. He filled his lungs with air. Then he took the regulator out of his mouth and handed it to Matt. Had he taken enough air in to last until Matt passed the regulator back to him? Matt took a deep breath of air and passed the regulator back to Josh. They continued to share Josh's tank of air as they rose to the surface of the water.

"Good job, guys!" Chris congratulated. "You've got the hang of buddy breathing. I think you're ready for your first open-water dive."

Those were the words Josh had been waiting all summer to hear. He'd already passed the written test. A real ocean dive would mean that he would soon be a certified scuba diver. His dad had promised to take him diving in the San Juan Islands off the coast of Washington as soon as he received his scuba certification, or "C" card.

Josh swam to the side of the pool. He reached down to remove his fins before climbing up the ladder. He slid his tank off and set it on the deck.

Matt joined him. "That was awesome!" he said, grinning.

"Yeah," Josh agreed. "But try not to hog all my air next time!"

Josh couldn't wait to tell his dad the good news at dinner that night.

"Dad, my scuba instructor says I'm ready for my first open-water dive. The class is going to dive under the old ferry dock at Logan Beach this Saturday."

"That's great," his dad replied. "Sounds like I'd better get down to the dive shop and book us that trip to the San Juans. Still interested?"

"You bet," Josh said.

He just hoped his dad wouldn't be disappointed having him as a diving buddy. After all, his dad had been a Navy Seal diver. How could Josh ever hope to measure up?

9
Night Dive

Four weeks later, Josh and his dad boarded
the ferry that would take them to the San Juan
Islands. The two leaned over the ship's railing. They
watched the scenery as the ferry slowly made its way
through the maze of islands that dotted the northern
tip of Washington.

"You know, Josh," his dad said, "the San Juan Islands have some of the best cold-water diving in the world. I think we'll probably see some eels and maybe an octopus or two. Keep an eye out. You might even see a killer whale."

Josh grinned. The only time he'd seen his dad this excited was at one of Sean's basketball games.

"Hey, Dad, there's a whale now," Josh teased. He pointed to a large gray object in the distance.

It was one of the navy's submarines. They sometimes did maneuvers near the base in Puget Sound.

"That's better than a whale. That's one of the navy's finest ships. I served on a sub just like that one in Hawaii," Mr. Scoville said proudly. He put his arm across his son's shoulders. The two of them watched the submarine move swiftly through the water.

"Pretty fantastic view, isn't it?" A voice from behind them asked. "Just wait until you see what's underneath the water."

Josh turned around to see Chris, his scuba instructor. He often led these diving trips to the islands on the weekends.

"Hey, Josh. I came to tell you and your dad that the group is getting together right now in the lounge. We're going to make plans for the weekend."

"Sure thing." Josh and his dad gathered their gear and followed Chris.

"Okay, everyone," Chris greeted. He walked over to the group of divers sitting on benches in the ship's front lounge. "Let's get to know one another and talk about how the weekend is going to go. As most of you know, I'm Chris. I'll be the lead instructor for our dives."

They went around the circle introducing themselves. A gray-haired man in a faded red T-shirt spoke first.

"I'm Ray. I live in San Diego, but I've been visiting my sister in Seattle. I thought since I was in the area, I'd check out the San Juans. I make my living diving off oil rigs, so I've been all over the world—or underneath it anyway."

Everyone laughed.

"But I've never been up here," Ray added.

"My name's Scott," said the blond, curly-haired guy sitting next to Ray. "I'm a student at the university. I've done some diving at a resort in Mexico. That's about it."

The college student nodded at Mr. Scoville, who introduced himself and Josh. A young married couple from Canada and two middle-aged women completed the group.

With introductions finished, Chris took over. "We're going to make our first dive tonight out in the harbor. We'll enter the water right from the beach next to the dock. For those of you who have never done it before, night diving is amazing. You'll see lots of fish that hide during the day. It's the best time to see an octopus. They're generally pretty shy creatures. You'll also notice that the phosphorous in the water will give everything a cool greenish glow.

"Tomorrow will be our big day," he continued. "We'll take a boat out to Sir Walter's Wall. It's a spectacular cliff." He saw a look of confusion on Scott's face. "An *underwater* cliff."

The group of divers nodded their understanding.

"It starts at around 25 feet under the water and drops straight down to 150 feet. We won't go down that far though. We'll be diving at around 90 feet.

"The wall is covered with giant anemone and some of the biggest barnacles in the world. You'll also see lots of rock fish. We won't be able to stay down there too long, but I promise you'll see plenty."

Chris finished. "Okay, the ferry's about to dock. Grab your gear. The hotel is at the top of the hill. We'll meet back at the dock at 8:00 tonight."

Josh and his dad walked off the ferry and climbed the hill to their hotel. The town of Rock Point Harbor was a quaint little fishing village. Everything centered around one main street. Josh looked around and saw a bookshop, an old movie theater, a small grocery store, and a dive shop. Fred's Friendly Café connected to the hotel.

"Doesn't look like much happens here," Josh said to his dad.

"Not on land anyway."

After settling in at the hotel, they decided to eat an early dinner at Fred's. They were nearly finished with their burgers when Ray and Scott walked in.

"Mind if we join you?" Ray asked.

"No, please do," Josh's dad replied. He slid over in the booth to make room.

The conversation quickly turned to diving. Mr. Scoville turned to Ray. "It must be interesting work diving on those oil rigs."

"The work is okay, but I do get to dive in some great waters. My last job took me to the Middle East."

"Aahh . . . the Red Sea." Mr. Scoville nodded knowingly. "I've heard the diving there is spectacular."

"Some of the finest," Ray agreed. "The coral reefs are gorgeous. So far they haven't suffered too much damage from pollution or tourism."

"I saw some awesome coral in Mexico," Scott interrupted. "I even snagged a piece to give my girlfriend." He grinned.

"Isn't that illegal?" Josh burst out. When he'd written his term paper, he'd learned that coral reefs were disappearing at an even faster rate than the rain forests. Some of the worst destruction was from tourists who didn't realize how fragile coral can be. They would carelessly trample a reef or break off bits to take home as souvenirs.

"It was just a little piece," Scott mumbled sheepishly.

"One that took 50 years to grow," Ray pointed out.

"Well, folks," Mr. Scoville said, changing the subject, "we'll see you guys at the dock in a little while." He and Josh scooted out of the booth.

At 7:30, Josh and his dad grabbed their duffel bags full of scuba equipment and headed down the hill. The bags were heavy. Scuba diving sure involves a lot of equipment, Josh thought as he lugged his bag to the dock.

Chris was already down at the beach laying out the air tanks. Other members of the group were trickling down slowly. Mr. Scoville laid out the equipment he and Josh would need for the dive.

His dad untangled the hoses that would connect to the air tanks. Josh cleaned their masks and sorted their fins. They also each had a weight belt and a Buoyancy Compensator, or BC. The BC was like a life vest that inflated either automatically or by blowing it up like a balloon. It helped the diver stay afloat on the surface of the water.

Josh stripped down to his bathing suit. The chill in the August night air hinted that fall was not far away. He quickly tugged on his wet suit.

Josh shivered. He didn't know whether it was from nerves or the cold night air. This was only the second time he'd ever done an open-water dive. And he'd never gone underwater at night.

Josh tried to hide his nervousness from his dad. He knew his dad wouldn't put up with any fear.

"Chilly, isn't it?" asked his dad.

Josh just nodded.

Together they checked their equipment. His dad opened and closed the valves on the air tanks. He scanned the O rings carefully for cracks. Josh knew that those little rubber rings could cause big problems underwater if they were cracked. He was relieved that his dad was inspecting their equipment. It made him feel a little safer.

"How are you doing, Josh?" his dad asked as he helped him adjust his BC.

"Okay." Could his dad see the knots in his stomach?

"You'll do fine. Diving is very safe as long as you focus and stay calm. Whatever you do, don't panic."

Josh thought about those words as his dad helped him put the air tank on his back and adjust his weight belt.

Chris came over to the group. "How's it going? I've already placed the red flag in the harbor to mark our dive site. Go on in when you're ready. Remember, you need to stay with your buddy at all times.

"We won't be diving deeper than 50 feet, so our dive tables allow us to stay down for 75 minutes. Set your watches. I'll see you at the bottom."

From his scuba diving class, Josh knew the importance of checking the dive tables. The tables calculated how long a diver could stay underwater at each depth. If you went too deep or stayed underwater too long, you could get sick or even die.

Mr. Scoville gave the instructor the thumbs-up sign. He looked at Josh. "Ready?"

"Yep," Josh replied.

Walking with fins was awkward. It was actually easier to walk backward. Slowly, they entered the water.

Josh gulped. The cold water filling his wet suit shocked his system. Once the thin layer of water between his skin and wet suit warmed up, Josh knew he would feel more comfortable. Those first few minutes, though, took his breath away.

His dad put his regulator in his mouth. He gave Josh a thumbs-up signal and dove beneath the surface. Josh followed. With their high beam flashlights leading the way, they saw an underwater world of wonder. Fish swam by, leaving a phosphorous trail of glowing green sparks. Every once in a while, his dad would tap Josh on the shoulder. He pointed out sea slugs and purple starfish. They saw anemones that looked like beautiful underwater flowers with their tentacles gently waving. Once, an octopus silently glided by with an eight-pronged phosphorous tail.

Now Josh understood why his dad loved scuba diving so much. No longer nervous, Josh enjoyed sharing the underwater world with his dad.

Suddenly Josh shot up to the surface. His BC was fully inflated. He began bobbing on top of the water.

His dad quickly followed. "What's wrong?" he asked.

"I don't know," Josh said, confused. "My BC just suddenly inflated . . ." His voice trailed off.

"You must have accidentally pushed your power inflator button." His dad sounded annoyed. "We might as well just call it a night."

Mr. Scoville couldn't hide his disappointment at having to cut the dive short. On shore, they left a note for Chris and headed back to the hotel in silence.

10
Trouble Undersea

Brilliant sunshine bathed the divers the next morning as they boarded the boat. The sun seemed to melt the disappointment of the previous evening. Both Josh and his dad were in good spirits.

The dive boat, *Misty*, was a 36-foot cruiser with a dive platform off the back. Josh was relieved to see the platform. It meant that the divers could just step off the boat into the water rather than jumping overboard. Josh wouldn't have to worry about readjusting his mask and equipment while treading the choppy water.

Everybody boarded quickly and loaded their gear. Then the captain and his first mate untied the mooring lines holding the boat to the dock. The *Misty* was soon underway. She made good speed. Her bow plowed through the small choppy waves easily like a playful dolphin pushing a ball.

The first mate laid out a light breakfast of donuts, juice, and coffee. The group gathered around to eat and talk about last night's dive.

They compared stories about what they'd seen. Each diver tried to outdo the other. Josh felt left out. Since their dive had ended early, he and his dad hadn't seen as much as the others. He couldn't quite look his dad in the eyes. He was sure he'd see renewed disappointment there.

Josh moved away from the group and began sorting through their equipment. He tried to ignore the laughter coming from the others. His dad soon joined him and helped lay out their regulators and hoses.

Josh could hear Scott say, "You should have seen the eel that Ray and I saw. The teeth on that thing were huge. It was a moray for sure."

"There are no moray eels in these waters," muttered Josh to himself. He tightened the strap on his mask. Yeah, but at least Scott managed to stay down long enough to see an eel, a voice inside Josh answered.

Ray broke away from the group and came over to the two of them. He handed Mr. Scoville a cup of coffee. "Had to cut out early last night, eh? Too bad. Scott was right about one thing. You missed seeing the largest eel I've ever laid eyes on. Maybe you and I could be dive buddies this morning. Since you used to be a Seal, I thought you might want to explore the wall more than you'll be able to with your son."

"No, thanks. I'm going to dive with my son," Josh's dad replied. He shimmied into his wet suit and attached a dive knife to his ankle.

Josh walked away from the two men. The words stung in his ears. His dad probably *did* want to dive with Ray. But he felt obligated to stick with Josh.

Josh wandered up to the front of the boat and leaned over the railing. Every once in a while, salt water would rise over the bow and spray him. The salt stung his eyes, but the water felt good.

Josh thought about his dad's words. "Whatever you do, don't panic." Well, he had certainly panicked last night. Josh promised himself that whatever happened this morning, he would stay calm.

Chris motioned for Josh to join him and the captain at the wheel. "I thought you might want to check out these navigational maps. Sailors call them *charts*. I always find it interesting to see where we're headed. At the moment, we're right here between these islands. See?" Chris's finger pointed to a thin body of water on the chart.

"We'll be moving through this channel soon." He traced their path on the chart. "The captain has to be careful motoring through the channel because it gets very shallow and there are a lot of rocks. See those buoys out there in the middle? They mark the safe area. We'll go around the head of that island into a bit of open water. Then we're at Sir Walter's Wall."

Chris put his hand on Josh's shoulder. "Hey, don't feel too bad about last night. It happens to all of us at one time or another. We all panic a bit when we're just starting out. I remember one of the first times I went diving with my dad. I kept thinking that my tank was leaking. It seemed to me like there were too many bubbles coming out. It turns out I was just breathing too fast because I was nervous. I was using up all my air. I made my dad cut the dive short. He wasn't too pleased with me." Chris shook his head.

"Just remember to stay calm," he advised. "You were a great student in class. In fact, you were one of the best. I wouldn't let you dive today if I didn't think you were ready."

The captain turned to Chris. "We're approaching the dive site." He cut the engine. While the captain and first mate anchored the boat, Chris called the group together.

"We're just about ready to dive," he told them. "I want to remind you to stay close to your buddy. The current can be quite strong along this wall. I'm going to throw a drift line down over the side of the boat. Just hold on to it as you go down the wall.

"I don't want anyone to get separated," Chris continued. "Watch out for kelp. It's a mess if you get tangled up in it. Everyone set your watches. Remember, we'll be going down to 90 feet, so we'll have only 30 minutes underwater this morning. Anyone have any questions?"

They all shook their heads. "Okay. Have a great dive," Chris said.

The first mate threw out the red and white dive flag to mark the diving spot. Boaters would know to stay clear. The divers could easily spot the flag from underwater so they'd know where the boat was.

He also threw down the drift line, a long rope attached to the boat. The divers could use it to guide themselves down the wall.

Josh and his dad stepped off the platform at the back of the boat. Josh had never been down to 90 feet before. His father assured him that it was no different than diving down to 35 feet.

"You just need to be aware of the time," he'd explained. "You'll be using up the air from your tank more quickly."

Josh and his dad took hold of the rope. Following Chris's lead, they kicked their fins and swam down through the cold, murky water. Josh was disappointed not to be able to see much sea life. Quickly he gave up trying to see anything. Instead he used the descent to get used to the water temperature and even out his breathing.

Suddenly the huge wall loomed in front of them. Chris pointed it out. The divers hugged the wall as they made their way slowly down the cliff. The careful movements of the group reminded Josh of rock climbers scaling a mountain. But these divers were intent on moving down the face of the rock, not up it.

Josh looked at his depth gauge. They were already at 60 feet. His breathing had the slow, rhythmic pace of an experienced diver. Josh was amazed at the quiet, dazzling world that lay before him. Mesmerized, he watched a school of rock cod swim in and out of nooks and crannies in the cliff.

Giant anemone covered the wall in a brilliant display of orange, purple, and white.

Josh pointed to an octopus that was squeezing inside one of the rock crannies. His dad nodded excitedly. For almost 20 minutes, they explored the wall. They were careful to watch that the current didn't carry them too far away from the group. All too soon, his dad gave the signal that it was time to head up.

Suddenly Josh noticed that Ray was caught in a mass of long, twisted kelp strands. The harder Ray tried to free himself, the more entangled he became. Ray was an experienced diver, but he had never encountered a kelp bed before. He didn't know that the long, slippery strands can wrap around a person tightly, making escape almost impossible.

Josh grabbed his dad and pointed to Ray. Together they swam over to the struggling diver. Mr. Scoville took out his knife. He began cutting away at the slippery strands of kelp. After what seemed like an eternity, Ray was freed.

Ray checked his air gauge. It was almost empty. He had used up too much air in his struggle to free himself from the kelp. Scott would have to buddy breathe with him to the surface.

Using hand signals, Josh's dad asked, "Where is your buddy?" Ray looked around uncertainly. Then he pointed upward.

Mr. Scoville started swimming toward Scott. The college student had panicked. Instead of helping his buddy, Scott had taken off. He'd quickly shot to the surface—*too* quickly. Now he was in distress at the surface.

Josh knew that Ray was low on air. The only way he would make it to the top was if Josh shared his air. For a moment, Josh hesitated. Ninety feet was a long way to the surface. Air was precious at this depth.

But Josh knew what he had to do. He took his regulator out of his mouth and passed it to Ray. They passed the regulator back and forth. Each diver filled his lungs with air before passing it to the other. Slowly they made their way up to the ocean's surface.

Once on top of the water, the other divers helped them aboard the boat. Ray was a little shaken, but otherwise he was fine.

Scott wasn't so lucky. He had risen too quickly. In his panic, he had held his breath. Now he was lying on the boat deck unconscious. Josh's dad was performing CPR.

Meanwhile, Chris radioed the Coast Guard. "We have a medical emergency here. One of our divers has decompression illness."

He turned to Mr. Scoville. "They're sending a helicopter. They'll take Scott to the decompression chamber in Seattle."

The helicopter arrived a few minutes later. It hovered over the small dive boat. A sling was lowered down. Chris and Mr. Scoville placed Scott in the sling. Chris motioned for the pilot to pull up. Soon Scott was safely inside the helicopter. The pilot pulled away.

"Is he going to be okay?" Josh asked as the noise from the helicopter died down.

"Yes, he'll recover. Decompression illness is serious though. It's hard on your heart and nervous system when you rise too quickly from so deep underwater. The decompression chamber will help get rid of the extra nitrogen in his body that couldn't escape when he surfaced."

Ray approached Josh and his dad. He offered his hand to Josh.

"Thanks," he said, shaking Josh's hand. "You saved my life. I was wrong about your diving skills. If you hadn't shared your air, it might have been me making the trip to the chamber. You can be my dive buddy anytime."

"Only when he's not diving with me," said Josh's dad proudly.